COCK-A-DOODLE-DOO!

by Jill Runcie · illustrated by Lee Lorenz

SIMON & SCHUSTER BOOKS FOR YOUNG READERS

Published by Simon & Schuster
New York • London • Toronto • Sydney • Tokyo • Singapore

SIMON & SCHUSTER BOOKS FOR YOUNG READERS
Simon & Schuster Building, Rockefeller Center, 1230 Avenue of the Americas, New York,
New York 10020. Text copyright © 1991 by Jill Runcie. Illustrations copyright © 1991 by
Lee Lorenz. All rights reserved including the right of reproduction in whole or in part in
any form. SIMON & SCHUSTER BOOKS FOR YOUNG READERS is a trademark of Simon & Schuster.
Designed by Lucille Chomowicz
Manufactured in Hong Kong   10 9 8 7 6 5 4 3 2 1

Runcie, Jill. Cock-a-doodle-doo! Summary: Farmer Jones's snores set off a series of
hooting, oinking, neighing, and barking, until the rooster's cock-a-doodle-doo wakes
him up. [1. Animal sounds—Fiction.   2. Farm life—Fiction.]   I. Lorenz, Lee, ill.
II. Title. PZ7.R88825Co   1991   [E]—dc20   90-35721
ISBN 0-671-72602-1

For Bix, Lulu and especially Lee — JR

Every day, Farmer Jones worked on his farm.

Every night, he slept soundly, knowing that
the rooster would wake him the next morning.

But the rooster slept soundly, too, knowing that
before sunrise Farmer Jones' loud snores...

would wake the owl sleeping nearby.

The owl would hoot and…

wake the sleeping woodpecker.

The woodpecker would peck…

and wake the sleeping duck.

The duck would quack…

and wake the sleeping frog.

The frog would croak…

and wake the sleeping pig.

The pig would oink…

and wake the sleeping lamb.

The lamb would baa…

and wake the sleeping horse.

The horse would neigh…

and wake the sleeping cow.

The cow would moo…

and wake the sleeping cat.

The cat would meow…

and wake the sleeping dog.

The dog would bark…

and wake the sleeping rooster.

The rooster would cock-a-doodle-do *sooo* loud…

that Farmer Jones would wake up,

jump out of bed and say...

"I don't know what I'd do without that rooster!"

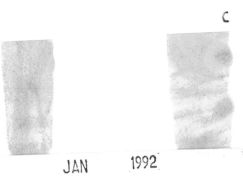

M031399736

RUNCIE, JILL

COCK-A-DOODLE-DOO

E   C

JAN   1992

CHESTERFIELD COUNTY LIBRARY
CHESTER

Regular loan: 2 weeks
A daily fine is charged for each overdue book.
Books may be renewed once, unless reserved for
another patron.
A borrower is responsible for books damaged
or lost while charged on his card.